W9-BYP-454

To Alun, with love, Jane

Barclay, Jane, 1957-
How Cold Was It?
Text copyright © 1999 by Jane Barclay
Illustrations copyright © 1999 by Janice Donato

Published by
Lobster Press Limited
1250 René-Lévesque Blvd. West, Suite 2200
Montréal, Québec H3B 4W8
Tel. (514) 989-3121 • Fax (514) 989-3168
www.lobsterpress.com

Edited by Jane Pavanel

Canadian Cataloguing in Publication Data

ISBN 1-894222-03-2

I. Donato, Janice Poltrick   II. Title

PS8553.A7432H68 1999   jC813'.54   C99-900678-9
PZ7.B236Ho 1999

Printed and bound in Canada

How Cold Was It?

Written by
Jane Barclay

Illustrated by
Janice Donato

Lobster Press Limited

When I woke up this morning
it was very cold.

How cold was it?

It was a **freezing,
     sneezing,
         goose-bumpy,
             teeth-chattering,
can't-get-out-of-bed,
         blankets-over-my-head**
                 kind of cold.

Outside, little brown birds huddled at the top of my neighbor's chimney, trying to keep warm. I lay in bed and listened to the wind whistle past. I watched as it shook the gray bones of the trees. During the night an ice fairy had sneaked through the crack in my window and sketched a magical picture of silvery leaves on the glass.

In the kitchen,
porridge bubbled,
coffee dripped
and my cat
threaded her way
between my shins.
"Mee-out, mee-out," she cried.
"It's too cold to go out, cat," I said.

How cold was it?

It was a **howling,
meowling,
fur-ruffling,
paw-shaking,
whiskers-in-the-breeze,
let-me-in-please**
kind of cold.

I sat at the table, poured milk on my cereal and sprinkled brown sugar on top. Out on the porch the wind whipped the snow into tiny white drifts, like meringue on a big frozen pie. Underneath the fir tree I spied a fat black squirrel trembling as it searched for buried seeds.

I could hear my dad trying to start the car.
He came in the front door, stamping the snow
from his boots.
"Man, it's cold out there," he said.

How cold was it?

It was a **car-wheezing,**
engine-seizing,
snow-shoveling,
ice-scraping,
temperature-falling,
taxi-calling
kind of cold.

It was time to go to school. I put on my snowsuit, hat, boots and mitts, then my mom wound a long scarf around my face. I trudged down the sidewalk, boots crunching in the snow. Steam rose from between the metal teeth of a sewer grate and I imagined a snow dragon awakened by the bitter cold. I broke some icicles from a fence and stuffed them down the grate. Frozen food for the hungry dragon.

In the schoolyard the swings rattled and snow hissed down the slide. The wind bullied me past the rink, where snow devils chased each other in an endless game of tag. Inside, we sat at our desks and the teacher said, "My, it's cold out there."

How cold was it?

It was an **ear-ringing,**
       cheek-stinging,
wet tears,
     dry cough,
        feet-are-froze,
so-is-my-nose
       kind of cold.

We went to art class and cut out giant snowflakes
and hung them up with string. In storytime
we read a book about Arctic explorers. During math
we filled in our thermometer charts and learned
all about minus.

When the last bell rang I braced myself for the walk home. I pulled my hat down over my ears, scrunched up my shoulders and opened the door. The cold pounced on me and licked at my face. I ran past the rink and the playground, my breath escaping in foggy clouds. I stopped at the sewer grate and peered into its frosty mouth. "Hellooo down there," I called to the snow dragon, then I hurried up the street. When I finally made it home my mom said, "Goodness, you look cold."

How cold was it?

It was a **hat-grabbing,**
scarf-nabbing,
nose-running,
lip-quivering,
both-ears-are-red,
numb-from-toe-to-head
kind of cold.

When I finished my snack my mom asked
me to get some bread from the freezer
for supper. Chills crept up my body as I headed
down the cold basement stairs.
I dashed across the icy floor and yanked
open the freezer door.
A blast of frigid air shot up my sleeves.
I grabbed the bread and raced
upstairs, the cold snapping
at my heels.

Late that night I lay under my blankets and listened as the spine of my house cracked and popped. I watched the stars shivering in the dark sky and thought of the snow dragon asleep in its cold winter bed. But my bed was nice and warm.

How warm was it?

It was a **snug-as-a-bug,**
big hug,
    wool socks,
      two quilts,
    fireplace heat,
      cat-at-my-feet
           kind of warm.